Dear Parent:
Your child's love of reading starts here!

Every child learns to read in a different way and at his or her own speed. Some go back and forth between reading levels and read favorite books again and again. Others read through each level in order. You can help your young reader improve and become more confident by encouraging his or her own interests and abilities. From books your child reads with you to the first books he or she reads alone, there are I Can Read Books for every stage of reading:

SHARED READING
Basic language, word repetition, and whimsical illustrations, ideal for sharing with your emergent reader

BEGINNING READING
Short sentences, familiar words, and simple concepts for children eager to read on their own

READING WITH HELP
Engaging stories, longer sentences, and language play for developing readers

READING ALONE
Complex plots, challenging vocabulary, and high-interest topics for the independent reader

ADVANCED READING
Short paragraphs, chapters, and exciting themes for the perfect bridge to chapter books

I Can Read Books have introduced children to the joy of reading since 1957. Featuring award-winning authors and illustrators and a fabulous cast of beloved characters, I Can Read Books set the standard for beginning readers.

A lifetime of discovery begins with the magical words "I Can Read!"

Visit www.icanread.com for information
on enriching your child's reading experience.

Epic: Meet the Leafmen
Epic © 2013 Twentieth Century Fox Film Corporation. All Rights Reserved. Printed in the United States of America. No part of this
book may be used or reproduced in any manner whatsoever without written permission except in the case of brief quotations embodied
in critical articles and reviews. For information address HarperCollins Children's Books, a division of HarperCollins Publishers, 10 East
53rd Street, New York, NY 10022.
www.icanread.com
Library of Congress catalog card number: 2012953623
ISBN 978-0-06-220993-1
Typography by Rick Farley

13 14 15 16 17 LP/WOR 10 9 8 7 6 5 4 3 2 1   ❖   First Edition

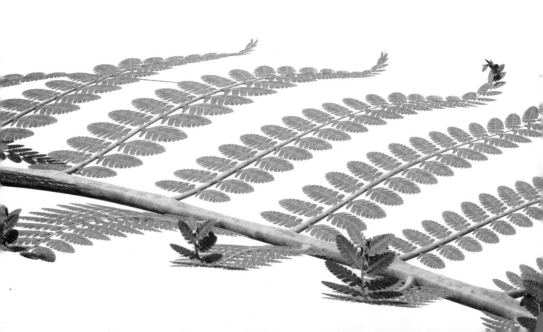

I Can Read!

READING 2 WITH HELP

Blue Sky studios.

epic

Meet the Leafmen

Adapted by Lucy Rosen

HARPER

An Imprint of HarperCollins*Publishers*

Deep within the forest,
between leaves and
blades of grass,
live the Jinn.

If you are careful,

you might see one.

But look closely!

The Jinn are tiny creatures.

Only two inches tall,

they are smaller than mice.

The Jinn are so little,

some even ride on hummingbirds

without being seen.

Some of the Jinn are warriors.

They are called the Leafmen.

They are guardians of the forest

and of their queen.

Quick and nimble,

the Leafmen are skilled fighters.

They wear armor

and carry swords.

The Leafmen vow
to protect their home
from the Boggans.
They are the Jinn's sworn enemies.

The Boggans are cold and cruel.

They want to destroy the forest.

Their poison arrows

make anything rot away.

The Leafmen won't let that happen!

Ronin is their tough leader.

He is serious, strong, and brave.

Ronin thinks that even though
each Leafman is different,
together they can help everyone.
"Many leaves, one tree,"
he always says.

Nod is also a Leafman,
but he is not like Ronin at all.
Nod does what he wants
and does not follow rules.

Some days,

Nod is not sure

he wants to be a Leafman

at all.

One day, the Jinn gather

for an important celebration.

Their queen is going to pick

the next heir for the forest.

THWACK!

Right after she chooses a pod,

an arrow flies overhead.

The Boggans leap

out of the woods!

The Jinn are under attack!

The Leafmen jump into action.

"Let's go!" Ronin calls.

"We must defend the forest!"

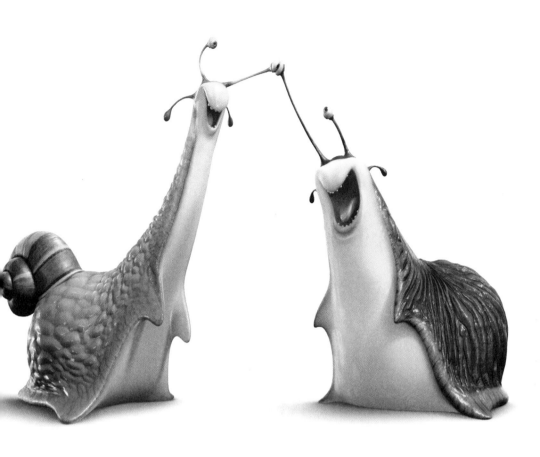

"We're ready!" cry two squeaky voices.

It's Mub and Grub,

a slug and a snail.

They are not Leafmen,

but they care about

protecting their home.

Nim Galuu also wants
to lend a hand . . . or six!
He is the oldest, wisest
caterpillar in the forest.
His scrolls contain many secrets.

One of his secrets

is how to keep

the queen's heir safe.

The pod the queen chose

will bloom in the moonlight.

"Count me in, too!" says M.K.

M.K. is a human.

She was magically shrunk

by the power of the queen

to help save the forest.

She was chosen by the queen

to keep the pod safe.

If she's with the pod when it blooms,

M.K. will be able to

return to her own world.

Ronin leads his friends

in the battle against the Boggans.

They fight as hard as they can.

But the Boggans are too strong!

Suddenly, a Leafman swoops in.

It is Nod!

He flies toward his friends

on his hummingbird.

Nod joins the battle.

He runs in, swinging his sword.

Ronin faces a fierce Boggan foe
and wins the fight.

Together with Nim, M.K., Mub, and Grub,
the Leafmen protect their home
with all their might.

At last, the Boggans give up.

"Retreat!" calls their leader.

They scurry away.

"We did it!" cheer Mub and Grub.

"Yes," says Ronin.

"Thank you for your help.

Nod, what made you change your mind?

I thought you didn't want to be

a Leafman."

Nod answered solemnly,

"Many leaves, one tree.

I might not like all the rules,

but we are all part of the same forest."

Ronin laughs.

"Now that sounds like

a real Leafman!" he says.